RUN, TURKEY, RUN!

Diane Mayr
Illustrations by Laura Rader

WALKER & COMPANY
New York

To all my writing buddies who never lost faith in my turkey story, and especially to Marty Darragh, who kept nudging me.
—D. M.

For Barbara and Bruce Sobol with many thanks.
Love, L. R.

First published in the United States of America in 2007 by Walker Publishing Company, Inc.
Distributed to the trade by Holtzbrinck Publishers

For information about permission to reproduce selections from this book, write to
Permissions, Walker & Company, 104 Fifth Avenue, New York, New York 10011

Library of Congress Cataloging-in-Publication Data
Mayr, Diane.
Run, Turkey, run! / by Diane Mayr ; illustrated by Laura Rader.
p.   cm.
Summary: The day before Thanksgiving, Turkey tries to disguise himself as other animals in order to avoid being caught by the farmer.
ISBN-13: 978-0-8027-9630-1 • ISBN-10: 0-8027-9630-3 (hardcover)
ISBN-13: 978-0-8027-9631-8 • ISBN-10: 0-8027-9631-1 (reinforced binding)
[1. Turkeys—Fiction. 2. Farm life—Fiction. 3. Thanksgiving Day—Fiction.]
I. Rader, Laura, ill. II. Title.
PZ7.M47375Run 2007   [E]—dc22   2006036190

The illustrations for this book were created with acrylic paint and ink on Strathmore bristol paper.
The text is set in Humana Sans, and the display type is Mod.

Book design by Nicole Gastonguay

Visit Walker & Company's Web site at www.walkeryoungreaders.com

Printed in Malaysia
10 9 8 7 6 5 4 3 2 1 (hardcover)
10 9 8 7 6 5 4 3 2 1 (reinforced)

All papers used by Walker & Company are natural, recyclable products made from wood grown in well-managed forests.
The manufacturing processes conform to the environmental regulations of the country of origin.

Turkey is having a terrible day.

It's the day before Thanksgiving,
but Turkey won't be giving thanks—
not unless he manages to escape.

Run, Turkey, run!

Clompity-clomp,
here comes the farmer!

Oh, see the pigpen?
If Turkey rolls in the mud,
will the farmer think he's a pig?

NO!
Run, Turkey, run!

Muckity-muck,
here comes the farmer!

Look, the duck pond!
If Turkey swims in the water,
will the farmer think he's a duck?

NO!

Run, Turkey, run!

Splashity-splash,
here comes the farmer!

Here's the place—the horse barn!

If Turkey sticks his head in the feed bucket,
will the farmer think he's a horse?

NO!
Run, Turkey, run!

Clankity-clank,
here comes the farmer!

Turkey can't fool the farmer.
He knows his animals!
What's Turkey to do?

Run from the farmyard!

Run, Turkey, run!

Crunchity-crunch,
here comes the farmer!

Hmmm . . . trees. If Turkey covers himself with branches, will the farmer think he's a tree?

Maybe . . .

The farmer doesn't see him.

Can it be?

Is Turkey safe at last?

YES!

Thanksgiving Day comes.

The farmer and his family eat peas, mashed potatoes, and grilled cheese sandwiches.

Turkey gives thanks!

Thanksgiving Day goes.

The farmer and his family are picking out their Christmas tree.

Run, Turkey, run!